STUBBY

MW01113738

Inspired by the True Story of an American Hero in World War I

By Kathy Borrus
Illustrated by Julia Mills

ISBN 9781790307883

Acknowledgements
Special thanks to Josh Finn, Diane Kidd, and Terrie Wolf.

An orphaned puppy wandered past a university stadium.
He was a curious stray with a tricolored coat,
a short tail, perky ears, and a square wrinkled jaw.
He was adventurous, but lonely. He wanted a friend.
So, one day he decided to go to college.
How would he get in?

He crawled under the fence and hid beneath the bleachers in the
university stadium. He slept there all night, alone.

The next day a tremendous noise woke him up.
He poked his head out to see what the commotion was all about.

It was a parade of students stomping in formation.
They were training to be United States soldiers.

The puppy ran out from under the bleachers and tried to march in step,
but the Sergeant chased him away saying,

"No dogs allowed!"

When the Sergeant wasn't looking,
the determined pup followed Private Conroy, all the way back to his dorm.
Surprised and delighted, Conroy picked up the little pup and asked,
"Do you have a name?"

Looking at the dog's stubby tail, Conroy declared,
"Stubby! That's what I'll call you."
Stubby was happy to have a name and a friend at last.

But pets were not permitted in the army.
Each day Conroy hid Stubby in his locker
with the lid propped up slightly. Would
anyone find him there?

One day, Stubby heard bugle calls.
Curious, he climbed out of the locker,
jumped through the open window,
and joined the marching soldiers.
The Sergeant was furious, but suddenly...

Stubby raised his paw and saluted the Sergeant!

"What a super dog!" Conroy shouted.

Everyone agreed, even the startled Sergeant.
And so, Stubby became the squad's mascot.

Finally, the day came when Conroy and Stubby had to ship out to war
aboard the USS Minnesota battleship, bound for Europe.
The ship's Captain, who didn't know Stubby was smart, said,
"No dogs allowed!" What would Conroy do?

When no one was looking,
Conroy tucked Stubby inside his coat
and boarded the battleship.

When the ship was too far away to turn back,
Conroy took Stubby out onto the deck.
The angry Captain said,
"That little stowaway goes as soon as we reach the shore!"

But by the time they docked in France, the Captain and the soldiers
all loved Stubby and did not want him to leave.
They even made him a set of dog tags.
Stubby joined Conroy and the troops in the trenches to keep them company.

Life in the trenches was hard and noisy.
The Americans were fighting the Germans.
"Rat-a-tat-tat, Rat-a-tat-tat."
The constant sound of machine gun fire hurt Stubby's ears
and the smell of gas hurt his nose.

The soldiers put on their gas masks, but Stubby didn't have one. He got very sick. Conroy rushed Stubby to the nearby field hospital.

When Stubby was better, the doctor said,
"Stubby should stay behind so he doesn't get hurt again."
Listening to the doctor, the Sergeant's voice boomed,
"No dogs allowed!"
"Let him try again," pleaded Conroy.

NO DOGS ALLOWED!

The Sergeant reluctantly agreed and outfitted Stubby with protective goggles. Stubby rejoined the troops. Late one night when the soldiers were all asleep, the Germans launched a massive attack. Uh oh.

This time Stubby's senses were on high alert.
"Arf, Arf, Arf," he warned as he ran through the trenches,
barking and nipping at the sleeping soldiers.

They woke up just in time to put on their gas masks.
Stubby saved the entire squad!

The next day Conroy and his company got lost
returning from a dangerous mission.

"Help, Help!" Conroy and the soldiers cried out.

With his keen hearing,
Stubby heard their cries.
He found Conroy and the others
and led them back to safety.

Stubby was so good at finding lost soldiers
that he went out on patrol every day. One time,
he heard a noise coming from a bush.
He sniffed around the bush and discovered...

A German soldier spying on the Americans!

"Grr, grr," growled Stubby and bit the spy on the backside.

For capturing the German spy,
Stubby was promoted to Sergeant!
Stubby now outranked Conroy.

The Germans were angry and they launched another attack.
Stubby stuck his head out of the trenches to look for injured soldiers.
Just then, there was a big explosion.

"Stubby!" Conroy shouted.
"Oh no! Stubby is wounded."

Conroy hoisted Stubby up into his arms
and raced to the field hospital.

While the doctors operated on Stubby, Conroy stayed by his side.

Would Stubby make it?

Stubby was a strong dog and he recovered.
As soon as he could get out of bed,
he trotted around the hospital
visiting other soldiers and making them happy.
He was the most popular patient in the hospital!

After the Americans won the war,
Stubby marched in a victory parade in Paris.
He met and saluted President Wilson.
One French lady even made Stubby a coat
for all the medals he won.

Back home in the United States, Stubby was greeted as a hero.
He visited the White House and led many
parades across the country.

And Conroy was always by his side,
best friends forever.

Kathy Borrus is the author of *Five Hundred Buildings of Paris*, *One Thousand Buildings of Paris*, *The Fearless Shopper*, and contributing essayist in *Fits, Starts & Matters of the Heart*. As former merchandise manager and buyer for the Smithsonian Institution Museum Stores, she was always inspired by museum exhibits where she first encountered Stubby's heroic story. This is her first children's book.

Julia Mills is an award-winning fine artist, illustrator, painter, educator, member of SCBWI, and enthusiastic knitter. Her work has been featured in knitting magazines and blogs. She brings her lively, painterly style to all her projects. This is her first children's book.

Made in the USA
Middletown, DE
22 December 2018